AN ILLUSTRATED GUIDE TO DRESSAGE

AN ILLUSTRATED GUIDE TO DRESSAGE

JENNIE LORISTON-CLARKE
and
CAROL WICKEN

PHOTOGRAPHS BY
BOB LANGRISH

THE STEPHEN GREENE PRESS
Lexington, Massachusetts

Text copyright © Jennie Loriston-Clarke and Carol Wicken, 1987
Photographs copyright © Bob Langrish, 1987
Diagrams copyright © W. A. Arnold, 1987
All rights reserved

First published in Great Britain in 1987 by Pelham Books Ltd.
First published in the United States of America in 1988 by
The Stephen Greene Press Inc.
Distributed by Viking Penguin Inc., 40 West 23rd Street,
New York, NY 10010.

CIP data available
ISBN 0-8289-0662-9

Printed in Great Britain
by BAS Printers Limited, Over Wallop, Hampshire
Filmset in Monophoto Ehrhardt

CONTENTS

INTRODUCTION

The aim of this book is two-fold. It can be used either as a guide by the knowledgeable spectator or it can be used to accompany existing instructional books by providing an extensive range of photographs.

There are plenty of very good training manuals available. Most of them are illustrated with drawings and very often good, but not enough, photographs to paint a clear visual picture of the text. By and large there is a dearth of good dressage photography, particularly showing work at the lower levels. This is principally because it is not an easy sport to capture on film and often produces shots of awkward moments in a movement. Writers conscious of a shortage of space choose the same type of photograph over and over again to illustrate articles. These usually show off the horse and rider to best advantage, but do not necessarily throw much light on the movement being performed. Among the selection we have chosen are some unusual shots including aerial views and a number of sequences.

Technical detail has been kept to a minimum and therefore descriptions of aids and training programmes have been left out, with the exception of a few general principles. Our aim is to keep explanations simple to avoid getting the reader bogged down with technical detail.

One always has to be careful not to be distracted from the ultimate aim of dressage which is to produce an equine gymnast going about his work with a spring in his stride, willingly carrying out the instructions of the rider, not resentfully going through the motions. Today more than ever when increasing prestige and prize money hang on competition wins the words of ancient horse trainers are as appropriate as ever. In his book written in 380BC the Greek statesman and general Xenophon said: 'Anything forced and misunderstood can never be beautiful.' He also quotes an earlier horseman Simon: 'If a dancer was forced to dance by whip and spikes he would be no more beautiful than a horse trained under similar conditions.'

Hopefully this book will be of interest to those with considerable knowledge as well as to those just beginning to take an interest. As a result of examining the photographs the latter group should be able to recognise the movements and degree of perfection. This increased understanding should in turn add to the reader's enjoyment of each performance viewed. With luck this will spark a desire for further investigation – and we will have another convert.

CHAPTER 1

THE EQUINE STARS

Three of Jennie's competition horses are used as models for this book.

Most senior is Dutch Courage who needs no introduction. This Dutch bred stallion, jointly owned by Jennie and Mrs R. Steele, was aged sixteen when these pictures were taken. He is now retired from competition work but during an illustrious dressage career represented Britain on numerous occasions. The highlight was his third place in the World Championships at Goodwood in 1978. To add to this he was six times National Champion and five times Dressage Horse of the Year. He is a half thoroughbred and the sire of many competition winners among them the two other horses used in the photographs.

Dutch Gold is a three-quarter thorough-bred stallion who was nine years old when the photographs were taken. This versatile horse is best known for his dressage wins which include a second in the Intermediare I at the Aachen CDIO against many of Europe's top international dressage horses. But he has also been Novice Horse Trials Champion and Open Spillers Combined Training Champion. His dam is Gold K who is also the dam of Tenterk, four times Hack of the Year.

DUTCH COURAGE	MILLEROLE T.B.	COBALT T.B.	TELEFERIQUE
			ALIZARINA
		MUSCIDA T.B.	BARNEVELDT
			MACKWILLER
	HIGONIA	AVENIR (Geld.)	KAROLUS VAN WITTENSTEIN
			RONNY
		CIGONIA (Gron)	PEPIJN
			NIGONIA

DUTCH GOLD	DUTCH COURAGE	MILLEROLE T.B.	COBALT
			MYSCIDA
		HIGONIA	AVENIR (Geld.)
			CIGONIA (Gron.)
	GOLD K T.B.	GOLDEN CLOUD	GOLDEN BRIDGE
			RAIN STORM
		CYRELLA	PHIDEAS
			ROYAL PALLETTE

Jennie favours the three-quarter thoroughbred for dressage because of the elasticity of paces, conformation and temperament that this type possesses.

FIG 1 Dutch Gold.

FIG 2 Dutch Courage (John Bunting).

Another fine example of the three-quarter-bred is Catherston Dutch Bid. He is the youngest of the three and was only six years old when these pictures were taken.

This young gelding, out of Night Auction, by Evening Trial, out of Eve by Fair Trial has exceptional paces and has done well in the show ring as well as the dressage arena. As a result he appears in the majority of our photographs, particularly where it is necessary to show clearly defined variations of pace.

CATHERSTON DUTCH BID			
DUTCH COURAGE	MILLEROLE	COBALT
		MUSCIDA
	HIGONIA	AVENIR
		CIGONIA
NIGHT AUCTION	EVENING TRIAL	FAIR TRIAL
		EVE
	MARKET FORTUNE	FORTINA
		MARKET DEAL

FIG 3   Catherston Dutch Bid.

CHAPTER 2

GENERAL PRINCIPLES OF TRAINING

As soon as the young horse is put into training he immediately has the problem of re-establishing his balance. When the horse is running free his weight is distributed more on the forehand than the quarters, the addition of a rider increases the problem.

He quickly learns to carry the weight of the rider, but if he is to undertake dressage training this is only the tip of the iceberg as far as work on his balance is concerned. Balance is only one of the slightly abstract concepts, highlighted in the next few pages, that play a vital role in training the horse to Grand Prix level. These are concepts that must be thoroughly understood before undertaking the training of the horse to the highest degree. They need to be described briefly to the reader about to embark on an introduction to the paces and movements.

The correctness of the final performance depends on rhythm, tempo, impulsion and the relationship they have with each other. The correctness of all future work depends on the foundations.

Returning to balance, we are continuously working on the balance of the horse and encouraging him to carry more of his own and the rider's weight on his hindquarters.

We achieve this by asking him to step further and further under himself with his hind feet, until we have extreme collection as in the piaffe. But on the other hand the horse needs to be versatile enough to extend or execute difficult transitions.

Transitions between different paces play an important part in developing this balance during the early stages. Once the horse has learnt to carry the rider it is important to get some rhythm into the work. Rhythm means the regularity of each pace; the regular 1-2-3-4 of the walk, 1-2 1-2 of the trot and the 1-2-3 of the canter.

Maintenance of good rhythm is the first indication that the horse is in balance, it also induces calmness. The rhythm must be maintained on both straight lines and through corners. In all paces the rhythm should remain the same. Tempo on the other hand is the speed of the rhythm and depends on the variation of pace. Tempo is the time that it takes for the footfalls to take place.

Once a good rhythm is established the next goal is cadence. A lack lustre performance can have rhythm but to achieve cadence there must be clearly defined rhythm combined with energy. This energy is brought

about by impulsion which is the harnessing of active forward movement. It is important not to confuse forward movement with speed when considering the meaning of impulsion. The energy is harnessed and channelled into making the steps more active and elastic. In extended paces the steps become longer but without becoming hurried and losing the rhythm. In collection the steps are shorter but the harnessed energy is directed into making them more elevated.

Speed may be a by-product as a result of an increase in tempo but otherwise it does not concern impulsion.

The energy is created by the effect of the rider's seat and legs on the hindquarters, while the bit controls the energy. This relationship between hindquarters and the horse's mouth is better understood if we examine the cycle of the aids. The rider's seat and legs promote the muscular activity of the hindquarters, the energy flows forward through the horse's back and neck to the poll and the mouth where it is taken up and controlled by the rider's hand. The flow continues through the rider's body back to the horse via the back and seat.

For the cycle of the aids to be uninterrupted both horse and rider must be supple and relaxed. The horse must be mentally submissive and willingly carrying out the rider's requests.

Having examined the circle of the aids the meaning of two other phrases used in dressage circles 'being between hand and leg' and 'the aids going through' become clear. For the aids to go through the horse the back must be relaxed because it is the bridge between the forehand and quarters. When the circle of the aids is complete the horse is between hand and leg.

Suppleness is one of the long term aims of the training. During the early days the emphasis is on lateral suppling. We ask the young horse to describe simple turns and circles with – as near as possible – a uniform bend of his body. The degree of bend possible in the spine is a matter of debate, although some of the aerial shots in this book should be interesting to those trying to establish how much lateral flexion is possible.

When asking for turns it is important that the horse's hind feet step onto the track of the fore feet. Work on circles helps make the

horse straight. The young horse will generally favour one side and work on circles encourages him to stretch the muscles on the hollow side and ultimately to take up an even contact. However, work on straight lines must not be ignored. The horse should be ridden actively forward, the hind feet stepping onto the tracks of the fore feet.

Longitudinal suppling begins once a degree of lateral suppleness has been established. Ultimately we want the horse to, figuratively speaking, resemble a coiled spring. Or a different image is that of a fencing foil flexed against a wall. In practical terms we ask the horse to step further and further under himself raising the forehand and increasing the bend in his back, neck and poll. Repeated transitions from pace to pace promote this.

One of the areas that can harbour most resistance is the poll. If there is a barrier here the energy will not flow freely through the horse's body to the rider's hand. Much of it will be blocked, impeding the free forward movement and limiting the rider's ability to control it. If there is tension in the poll the

back will flatten. To rid his back and neck of tension the young horse is encouraged to stretch his muscles and is only gradually asked for increased flexion of the poll. As the forehand and neck rises it should be the poll that compensates by increased flexion and not the neck which bends.

When the horse's face is vertical we carelessly talk of him as being 'on the bit'. This is misleading because the horse is only truly 'on the bit' when there is an elastic contact between the horse's jaw, which is supple and flexing, and the supple wrist of the rider. Podhajsky* describes it thus: 'The rider should have the feeling that he is connected to the horse's mouth by means of an elastic ribbon.' The horse must be in absolute balance and self carriage not supporting himself on the reins. It is important to bear in mind these conditions before pronouncing him on the bit.

An obsession with the angle of the face has led some riders to force their horses to adopt

---

* Col. Alois Podhajsky, for many years director of the Spanish Riding School, Vienna,

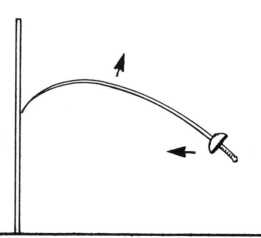

The impulsion from the quarters meets a restraining hand. The effect is to make the hind feet step further under the body and raise the forehand. This can be compared to a foil flexed against a wall.

an unnatural position. This can only lead to more problems in the long run. The correct angle of the face will only come about by increased flexion of the poll, which is the result of longitudinal suppling and suppleness of the jaw.

When the horse is between hand and leg work can begin on the half-halt, one of the most versatile and vital aspects of training but also one of the most difficult to grasp. At its most subtle it is barely discernible to the onlooker which makes it difficult to teach.

The half-halt can be used as a signal to a trained horse – to prepare him for a change of pace or direction; to re-establish balance, collection or impulsion; to stimulate or correct him. The half-halt consists of a forward urge by the seat and or legs that is caught by the hands. The hands prevent an increase in speed but allow the horse to step further under himself with a resulting lightening of the forehand.

The degree to which these combined aids are used depends on the state of training of the horse and what is being asked. In an advanced state it will be prompted merely by a bracing of the back. The hands doing no more than catch the increased impulsion, momentarily, then releasing to allow the horse to carry himself. Too much hand and the moment will be lost, restraining the forward movement and encouraging the horse to lean on the hand. Ultimately the half-halt will become second nature to both horse and rider.

The Walk

The walk is the most difficult pace to develop because of its complicated sequence of steps. The horse moves one leg after another so there is no moment of suspension to be lengthened or shortened.

Four hoof beats are heard and the sequence is for example left hind leg, left fore leg, right hind leg, right fore leg. The movement always begins with a hind leg and there are always two or three feet on the ground. The horse moves freely forward with even strides, the feet lifted purposefully and not dragged.

The sequence of steps remains the same throughout the variations which are collected, medium and extended walk. There is no working pace, the medium walk is used for initial training purposes.

FIG 4   In the medium walk the horse is coming from behind well, accepting the rein, with the nose in front of the vertical. The strides are free and energetic looking, although not as relaxed as in the free walk. The horse is supple and relaxed in the jaw, there is no resistance shown anywhere.

At the medium walk the horse should over-track – the hind feet touching the ground in front of the hoof prints of the fore feet.

The free walk is used as a reward for good work, it allows the horse to stretch out and is useful for combating tension and maintaining purity of pace. The horse is encouraged to take the bit from the rider's hand. This variation of the pace is used in competition to show the correctness of the work; in that the young horse is calm and relaxed. A tense nervous horse would not calmly take the bit.

FIG 5   The horse is in free walk, he has a contact and is seeking the rein. There is a feeling that he could take more rein which should be allowed to him. He has walked through well with the hind leg and is about to swing onto the near fore. The rider could have more weight in the stirrup, perhaps the rein could be a fraction longer and the elbow slightly more bent. However the rider has allowed him to take the rein and the elbow-bit line is nearly correct, although the hands could be a fraction higher.

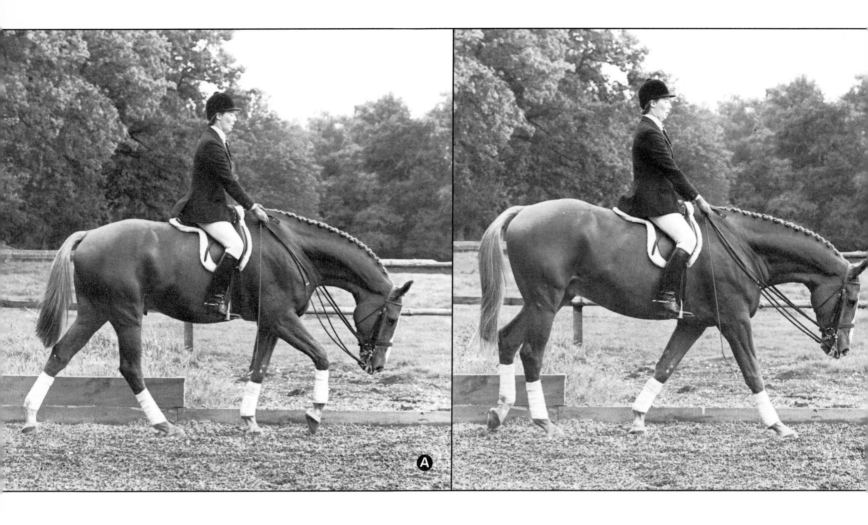

The free walk is used in two forms: on a long rein and on a loose rein. In figs 6a–d Dutch Bid calmly and confidently shows how it should be executed, taking the bit and stretching out and down, the steps long and swinging but not lazy.

FIG 6   This is a sequence of the horse taking the rein to allow a free walk on a loose rein. In (a) the rein is only just becoming loose and the horse is going forward well. The off hind is well under the horse and the off fore is going to march well forward. The steps are long and true in sequence. The rider's position is correct, still riding forward with seat and lower leg. (b) The off fore is on the ground and taking the weight as the horse swings over the shoulder to take the next step. In (c) we again see gravel in motion caused by the near fore that has left a spot midway between the two hindlegs. The horse is therefore over-tracking by about six to eight inches. His fore and hind feet are clear enough to avoid over stepping. In (d) the near fore has come well forward in true marching style. The position in this photograph is not to be confused with pacing. The diagonal pair of hind and forelegs are firmly on the ground, while the other two feet are either coming off or landing. The whole movement is in true four time beat with tremendous free forward movement.

The steps cover most ground in the extended walk, the rider allowing the horse to stretch his head and neck, lengthening his form but maintaining a contact. The extended walk is very difficult to master and even at Grand Prix level very few horses are capable of producing a true extension. It is important that the steps should not become hasty or the rhythm lost. It is very easy to let the horse quicken.

FIG 7   In the extended walk the outline is longer. The horse is going forward from the leg into the hand and accepting the bit. The nose is a little more in front of the vertical and the steps are lively and energetic. The rider has an incorrect leg position, her heel has come up instead of being down and riding the horse forward with seat and leg.

At the opposite extreme the same is true of the collected walk, when the horse is in his most compressed form, his steps more elevated and covering the least ground. If the horse is allowed to quicken this can develop into an amble (also known as 'pacing'). In extreme cases the two lateral pairs of legs appear to swing forward together and only two beats are heard. Normally each hind leg comes to the ground as its lateral fore leg lifts. There is a distinct 'V' shape formed by the angle of fore and hind leg. In the amble this 'V' disappears as the fore leg and hind leg on the same side become almost parallel.

FIG 8   This is a sequence of shots of the collected walk. In (a) the horse is walking energetically forward but is slightly running onto his forehand as the rider's driving and restraining aids are not quite 'through' enough. With a little more energy created by the lower leg the horse has become a little rounder in (b). But on putting the near fore to the ground in (c) the horse has come against the hand which has caused him to show resistance in the lower jaw and tension in the lower neck muscles. However in (d) the rider has softened the hand, the horse has softened the jaw and accepted the collected walk. In this picture he shows lively, energetic, high steps with a correct carriage and softness from the tail through his back to his poll and lower jaw.

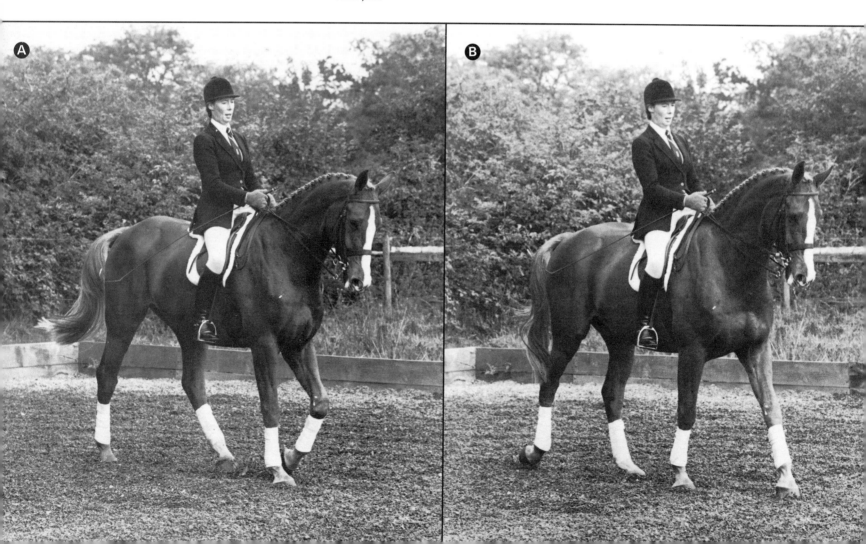

The Trot

The trot is the best schooling pace because of its symmetrical two-time movement, the horse springing from one diagonal pair to the other. The right fore leg and left hind leg leave the ground before the left fore leg and right hind leg touch and there is a split second of suspension that becomes more pronounced as the stride lengthens. The strides should be light and elastic, the hind feet stepping actively under the horse.

The trot is the easiest pace at which to establish rhythm (and eventually cadence) because of its regularity. It is also the most calming pace and the easiest at which to iron out faults, in turn improving the other paces. That is not to say that faults cannot develop at the trot. Those to watch out for are hurried steps of the fore legs, which can reach the ground before the diagonal hind leg. This throws the weight further on to the forehand exactly the reverse of what we are trying to achieve. In bad cases this can lead to two separate hoof beats instead of one. If the opposite is true and there is a hasty hind leg this reaches the ground before the diagonal fore leg. When this happens the hind leg does not step sufficiently under the body making what appears to be a longer stride with the fore legs. If the hind legs are not sufficiently engaged at the working and medium trot this can become a considerable fault when extension is asked for.

The working trot lies between the collected and medium paces and is the first to be developed from the horse's ordinary trot. At the working trot the horse is taught to engage his quarters for the first time, moving freely forward in a calm manner accepting the bit and contact with the rider's hand via the reins. The horse is asked to carry himself not support himself on the reins.

FIG 9 The horse is in working trot showing lively and energetic steps. He is tracking into or slightly over the print of the off fore. The horse shows a lot of energy from behind and appears a fraction overbent at this stage of the trot. But as the left fore actually hits the ground he will be in the correct outline, as the next diagonal pair of legs come through. It is extremely important that the working trot comes with energy from the hind legs and that the horse does not pull himself forward with the front legs and a hollow back.

Once the working trot has been established the rider can ask the horse to lengthen into the medium trot. This demands increased activity of the hindquarters but without allowing the horse to lose his rhythm and quicken. Instead there is a lengthening of the steps and an increase of the moment of suspension so that the hind feet over track the fore feet. The horse is allowed to lengthen his stride and outline to its full extent for the extended trot. The horse should be calm and unhurried with no loss of rhythm. The forehand should be light because of the increased carrying ability of the hindquarters. If the forehand becomes heavier the horse is losing his balance.

The strides are long and low, the opposite extreme of the collected trot. The lower part of the horse's leg is parallel with its diagonal partner and the feet of each pair reach the ground at the same moment. There should be no flicking of the fore legs. The horse is unable to place his fore legs beyond an imaginary boundary which follows the line of his face to the ground. If his legs are extending beyond this they will have to be withdrawn before touching the ground, thus producing a false extension. This shows the importance of allowing freedom of head and neck in extended paces.

FIG 10   Here in medium trot the horse shows a lively impulsion and enough energy coming from the hind legs to allow him to swing through with each diagonal pair of legs for a medium extension. The horse is in balance and lightly accepting the bit.

FIG 11   In the extended trot shown here the horse is showing maximum energy coming from the hind legs. The cannon bones of the near fore and off hind are at the same angle which demonstrates that the impulsion is coming through the horse from behind.

During the collected trot the steps are short, lively and elevated. The hoof prints of the hind feet fall into or behind those of the fore feet. The fore hand light with the quarters carrying even more of the load. The rider must be very careful that there is no loss of impulsion and rhythm in the collected trot, its mastery is the key to advanced movements such as piaffe and passage.

FIG 12   Collected trot. At the time these pictures were taken Dutch Bid was only a six-year-old so his performance in the collected trot is particularly good. He is actively coming from behind. All of the joints – hocks, knees and fetlocks – are bending well for the higher and shorter steps required. The muscles are working energetically from the quarters, through the back and neck in the collected outline. The rider is in the centre of the horse and the horse's balance is correct on the diagonal legs touching the ground.

The Canter

After the trot the next 'pace' is the canter which is a series of bounds, each made up of a three-beat movement followed by a moment of suspension.

In the canter right the horse is bent fractionally round the rider's right leg with his right lateral pair of legs stepping further forward than the left lateral pair, making them the leading legs. The sequence begins with the left hind leg forming beat one, the right hind and left fore together forming beat two, finally the right fore leg forming the third beat followed by a moment of suspension. The first hind leg should leave the ground before the leading fore leg touches.

For the left canter the right hind leg begins the movement, then the diagonal pair, finishing with the left fore forming the leading leg.

Common faults with young horses or those learning the flying change is the disunited canter, when the horse changes in front but not behind. As we have seen in the true canter the horse leads with the inside lateral pair of legs, in the canter right the right hind and right fore sweeping further forward. In the disunited canter (right) the diagonal pair (left hind and right fore will lead) making the canter appear lumpy and uncomfortable for the rider.

A false canter is when the horse is bent in the opposite direction to his leading legs. Even during the counter canter this is not correct as the horse is very slightly bent towards his leading legs, although away from the direction of movement.

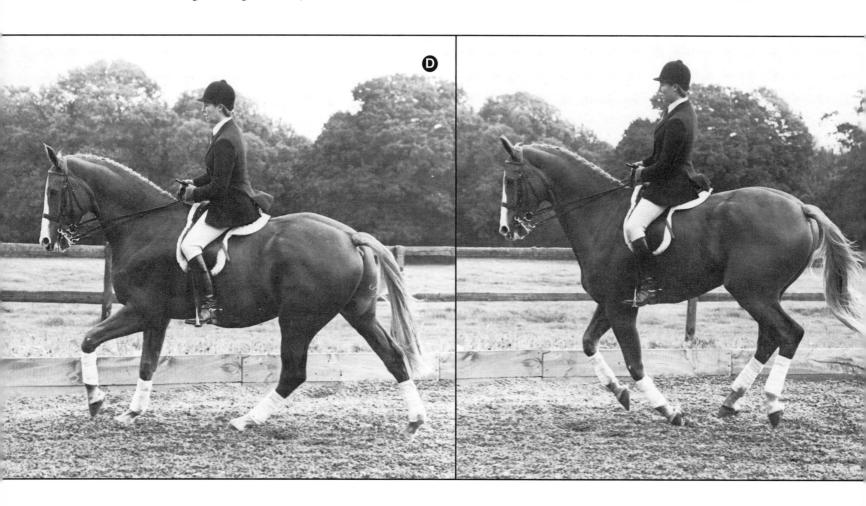

FIG 13　Here in (a) the horse is beginning in the working canter stride where he is propelled by the outside hindleg, taking all of the weight and lifting the forehand. He is in a nice rounded outline and the inside hind leg has come well under his body to take the weight of the next step. In (b) the weight is on the front legs making the horse appear overbent. It is the moment when the hind legs are about to come off the ground and the weight will come on to the near fore. The horse is accepting the rein well, with free forward movement. In (c) it is a split second before the moment of suspension when all four legs are off the ground ready to take up the position in (a). The horse is correctly balanced during this moment of the canter. In (d) you can clearly see the second stage of the canter when the diagonal has just come to the ground, soon to be followed by the near fore to take up the weight as in (b).

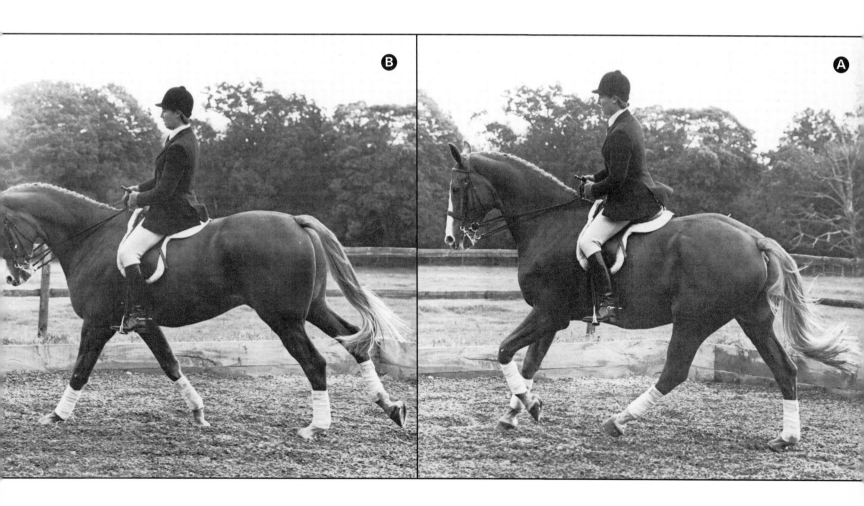

Having pointed out faults to watch for we move on to the variations of pace which are the same as for the trot; working, medium, extended and collected. There are the same basic requirements for balance, rhythm and length of outline. For the extended canter and to a lesser degree the medium canter there should be a lengthening of both stride and outline. The stride is shorter and bouncier for the working canter, the initial schooling pace, and still more so for the collected canter. In the collected canter the horse should resemble a coiled spring. As with the trot the moment of suspension doesn't alter, the steps become more elevated as they cover less ground.

FIG 14   In the canter viewed from the front the horse should be completely straight, although it is important to bear in mind that the shoulders are narrower than the quarters. You always have to consider the position of the shoulder in canter. You can see clearly that the horse is slightly in position right, with the rider's right leg on the girth and left leg behind the girth, riding the horse forward into the left rein, the right rein indicating the direction.

FIG 15 The canter viewed from behind shows the moment of suspension. It is difficult to tell whether the horse is going to land directly on the straight line. It appears that the quarters may be a fraction to the left, which would be corrected by the inside leg on the girth riding the horse into the right rein, bringing the shoulder slightly to the left.

FIG 16   The outline is slightly longer in medium canter and the steps energetic and well forward, with the impulsion coming from behind.

FIG 17   At this moment of the extended canter the horse is just beginning to put his weight onto the near hind just after the moment of suspension. The forehand is higher and lighter than the quarters. The nose is well in front of the vertical and the rider will allow the horse to lengthen his frame as he puts the diagonal (off hind, near fore) to the ground.

The canter is more difficult for the young horse because the uneven movement makes it more difficult for him to balance. There is horizontal movement in the horse's body a raising of the forehand and lowering of the quarters during beat one when the initiating hind leg comes under the horse. Then during beat three the forehand lowers and the quarters rise as the leading fore leg is the only one on the ground. If the movement is frozen at this point it appears awkward and the horse looks overbent. Because of this undulating movement the horse's head appears to nod, but this nodding should not be more than the corresponding movement of the body. Excessive nodding indicates lack of impulsion.

Another sign of lack of impulsion is a four beat canter when the diagonal pair which forms the second stage breaks up to form two beats. When this happens the lack of co-ordination between the diagonal pair may be very slight but is still wrong. In the four time canter the movement appears lumpy and can result from the rider asking for collection too soon before the other variations of the pace have been established or the hindquarters engaged.

During canter work three crisp beats should be heard and if they are not clearly definable things are beginning to go wrong. The importance of straightness has been stressed in other paces and applies no less to the canter work. Watch for the hind legs not following in the tracks of the fore feet. The young horse will often try to carry his quarters to the inside where they will avoid stepping under the body and developing the carrying power of the quarters.

In the counter canter the opposite is true, the horse may try to carry his quarters to the outside as he is bent to the outside of the circle. In a good counter canter the horse should be uniformly bent to the outside, that is on a left circle he will be bent to the right with the right lateral pair of legs leading. This is a useful suppling exercise which encourages the engagement of the hindquarters. It is also useful for teaching the flying change.

FIG 18   Again the horse is in the moment of suspension this time in collected canter. The rider is in an upright position to lighten the forehand. The horse is more rounded from his tail through his body and neck to his head, which is in a more vertical position. The steps have become shorter, rounder and higher showing a lively energy.

FIG 19   Here the horse is in counter canter, on the right rein in left canter. He is a little bit tight in the back and neck, tension is showing slightly in the lower jaw and neck muscles.

The Halt

The halt is often one of the most neglected areas of the horse's training. From the outset we should insist that the horse stands still while we mount. Unfortunately some people never establish this and, for many who do, work on the halt never progresses further.

A good halt demands as much attention as the other paces. When standing properly the horse should be square, i.e. carrying his weight evenly on all four feet. Ideally each pair should be in perfect alignment so that from the front, back and side views the horse appears to only have two legs. The horse should be lightly holding the bit and his overall appearance should be attentive, neither restless and fidgeting nor lazy and half asleep. He should be immobile but still in working mode, poised ready to step forward at the first indication and with his head held slightly in front of the vertical.

When stepping into the walk the horse should close into the walk from behind not be pulled into it from the front, harsh rein aids have no place in a good halt.

FIG 20   In the halt the horse's weight should be evenly distributed over all four legs. The horse should be ready and able to move off at the slightest application of the aids. Therefore he should remain quietly accepting the bit with a lively interest.

FIG 21   Seen from the front the halt should appear square, here the hind legs are a fraction wide. Although the horse is still on the bit it appears that his head should be a little lower.

FIG 22   This horse is a little more advanced. He is standing square on all four legs with a rounder and higher outline, ready to go forward into whatever pace is required. Note the quiet acceptance of the bit. The horse has a soft, wet mouth and the muscles are correctly placed for this moment of immobility. The poll is the highest point and the nose a fraction in front of the vertical.

The Rein back

If a correct halt is not established the rein back will not be performed properly. The rein back is forward movement caught by the rider's hands and directed into backward movement. For the rein back to be successfully taught the horse must be lightly on the bit with his quarters engaged. From the halt he will have to step forward but will be restrained by the hands and without hesitation step back into the rein back. After the required number of steps the hands allow him to go forward again, without hestitation.

The whole movement should be fluent, not broken into stages, with the horse relaxed and balanced throughout. There must not be any pulling on the reins as this only leads to tension and hollowing of the back. The horse is not pulled backwards but moves in that direction when he finds his way forward blocked by the rider's hands. When the obstacle is removed he immediately moves forward again. During the rein back the legs move in diagonal pairs similar to the trot but without the moment of suspension. The left fore and right hind move together and the right fore and left hind form a pair. The feet should be cleanly picked up and put down. It is theoretically a two beat movement, although it is a matter of discussion whether the legs of each diagonal pair should be put down simultaneously. Certainly for competition and according to the Federation Equestre Internationale guidelines it is acceptable if each fore leg is raised and reaches the ground 'an instant' before its corresponding hindleg.

When watching from in front and behind the horse should move straight, not evading to one side or the other. He should be on the bit and ready to move forward at any moment.

The rein back is not an easy movement for the horse whose propelling power is designed to come from the quarters. In the rein back it is reversed with the quarters leading the movement and the forehand responsible for the propulsion. The rein back is a useful step toward true collection because the horse is obliged to engage his quarters.

The Rein back

FIG 23   (a) Here the horse has been pushed with a stronger lower leg into a slightly restraining hand to produce the rein back. The rider's weight is slightly off the seat allowing the horse's back to come up and the horse steps backwards in diagonal pairs. The horse has accepted the restraining aids, his jaw is relaxed and his ears happy. He is about to move the left diagonal backwards. In (b) the diagonal pair of legs have been well picked up and are being taken backwards. The horse shows a little tightness in the neck muscles going into the lower jaw. The horse is taking the weight on his hindquarters and not too heavily on the front legs.

FIG 24   The rein back should be clear and straight when seen from the front or rear.

CHAPTER 4

DRESSAGE MOVEMENTS

Turn on the Forehand

The turn on the forehand is an exercise used by many trainers as an introduction to two track work. This exercise is performed by asking the horse to step sideways away from the rider's leg, at the same time catching and moderating the sideways movement with the other leg. The fore legs describe a small circle while the hind legs make a much larger circle round them.

If the rider asks the horse to move away from the left leg the horse's left hind will step sideways crossing in front of the right hind, the right leg steps away from it and the process begins again, the steps being of equal length. Meanwhile the front feet step up and down forming a very small circle.

The legs move in the sequence of the walk which is the only pace at which the exercise is performed. It can be started from halt or walk although once the basics have been learned the latter is preferable to avoid loss of impulsion.

During the movement the horse can be flexed in either the direction of the movement or more commonly away from it. For example the head and neck will be flexed and moving to the left while the hindquarters move to the right away from the left leg. Or in the counter pose, flexing to the right while the quarters move to the right. The pivot of the movement is the fore leg on the side to which the head is flexed.

The turn on the forehand is relatively easy for the horse because his weight is naturally on his forehand so it is easy for him to mobilise his quarters around them. This throwing the weight back on to the forehand is one reason why some trainers are against the use of this exercise. It is also difficult to maintain impulsion which can result in the horse stepping back and this should not be allowed under any circumstance. The turn on the forehand is a means to an end and should not be practised continuously. It is not included in tests for that reason.

Turn on the forehand

FIG 25   The horse has been in halt and has been asked to move his quarters round to the right, the forehand staying nearly on the spot but not pivoting. This is the beginning of the first step of the turn on the forehand. (b) Here the horse is about to cross the left hind in front of the right hind. (c) Moments later this is clearly seen.

Leg Yielding

Another exercise which is often used as an introduction to lateral work, but is not part of classical dressage, is leg yielding. The horse is asked to move diagonally forwards and sideways at either walk or trot. His body is straight although a slight bend is allowed to the outside, away from the direction of movement, so that the rider can see the eyebrow and nostril of the horse on the side of the bend. When moving to the left the right legs move in front and cross the left legs. It is often introduced to the horse at walk and when the lesson is understood it is better to work on the trot, where forward impulsion is easier to maintain.

Again this exercise is not popular with with many trainers. The argument is that it is inconsistent to teach a horse to move diagonally away from the leg, while bent away from the direction of movement when later on in half pass we will ask him to bend the opposite way.

Turn on the forehand and leg yielding are both only introductions to lateral work and do not deserve to be included under that heading. Only shoulder-in, travers, renvers and half pass are true lateral movements.

Leg Yielding
FIG 26 (a,b,c,)   The horse is yielding from the right leg and traversing sideways to the left keeping the body parallel to the side of the school. The horse has come from the right rein down the centre line. He is yielding from the right rein trotting forward and sideways to the left with a slight flexion to the right. The rider must be sure to ride the horse forward as well as sideways and to make sure the horse does not collapse on to his left shoulder.

The aim of this group of exercises is to increase the suppleness and mobility of both the shoulders and hindquarters. This in turn improves the balance, cadence and also obedience. During each movement there should be as near as possible a uniform bend from head to tail which is easier seen in the aerial shots.

For lateral work to begin the horse must have obtained a degree of collection, although this work has the effect of further improving collection.

Shoulder-in

The first movement to be taught is shoulder-in which is the backbone of all lateral training. The forehand is brought in about a quarter of a metre from the original track and follows on a separate but parallel track to the hindquarters at about thirty degrees to the direction of movement.

The inside fore leg passes and crosses the outside fore leg while the hind legs continue straight on. The inside hind leg steps forward under the horse towards the centre of gravity in turn helping achieve greater collection and suppleness. The forehand is taken in to the maximum degree possible so that the horse is still bent round the rider's inside leg, not merely proceeding with his whole body diagonally to the direction of movement when the back legs will begin to cross.

The number of tracks that should be seen when watching from the front is three. The two front legs and outside hind are visible and the inside hind is masked by the outside fore. The horse should of course perform the same degree of bend to each side. The greater the degree of bend the more the inside hind will step under the horse and the greater the freedom of the shoulders.

Shoulder In

FIG 27   Here the horse is ridden with the inside leg into the outside hand which has initiated bringing the shoulders off the track. The steps should be lively and the horse on three tracks with the inside hind and off fore on the same track.

To recap there must be no crossing of the hindlegs and the quarters must not be allowed to fall out but must continue unaffected on their original track.

The shoulder-in is performed almost exclusively at the trot, although the walk may be used in the early stages to teach the movement. It can be combined with the extended trot as a useful transition, moving out of shoulder-in across the diagonal in extension. This transition has the advantage of improving both movements. The shoulder-in can suffer from lack of impulsion in the early stages of being taught and the active forward movement of medium or extended trot helps overcome this problem. While the collected nature of the shoulder-in improves the subsequent extension. In the renvers and travers the horse looks in the direction of movement.

FIG 28 This shows from above how the horse's body bends in the shoulder-in, particularly when the inside hind is off the ground. The weight of the horse is on the right hind and left fore. You can see clearly the bend in the horse's body and neck with the shoulder being controlled by the outside rein.

FIG 29 (a,b,c,) This sequence shows the horse trotting with lively steps, showing a little bit of right bend through the trot with the steps active and coming well under the horse.

Travers

In travers, also known as quarters-in or head to the wall, the quarters are brought in towards the centre of the school (assuming that the movement is being performed along the long side) while the forehand continues along the track. As with the shoulder-in it is performed at the trot although can be introduced at walk. It is primarily an exercise to increase control over the hindquarters and is useful when combined in a sequence with shoulder-in (illustrated). Here the horse begins in shoulder-in and changes to travers via a ten-metre circle.

Like shoulder-in travers can be performed along the side of the wall or on the centre line. Despite its advantages travers has its critics who feel that it encourages inherent crookedness in the horse. Podhajsky claims to have used this movement infrequently at the Spanish Riding School.

Travers

FIG 30   Here the horse is trotting forward, the body bent round the right leg with flexion slightly to the right for the travers.

FIG 31   This frame shows the travers from behind. The four tracks of the movement are obvious, compared to the three tracks of the shoulder-in. There is a very clearly shown bend round the rider's left leg.

FIG 32   Here the horse is again bent round the rider's left leg bent toward the direction of movement. At this moment of the stride he is not showing much bend in his body.

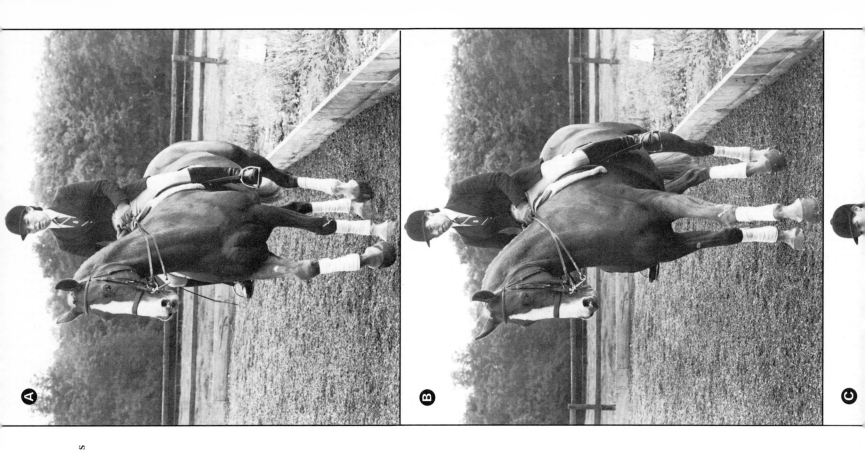

FIG 33   In this sequence the horse moves from shoulder-in to travers through a ten-metre circle. In the first photograph he is correct in shoulder-in.

In (b) the rider has just applied the aid to ride forward into the right circle.

By (c) the horse is one step into the circle, one stride later in (d) he is leaving the track and by (e) is directly on the circle.

In (f) the horse is coming out of the circle in right flexion. The left leg puts the horse in travers in which he stays calmly bent round the right leg accepting the bit and aids throughout.

Renvers

The renvers, also known as quarters-out or tail to the wall, is also designed to increase the rider's control over the hindquarters. It can be introduced from passada (from which it can later be used to teach pirouette), when coming out of a circle or when finishing a half pass. The renvers is performed at all three paces and its usefulness in teaching the pirouette makes it popular.

There is more collection required than for the shoulder-in, and the increase in control over the hindquarters is an important step in preparing for the half pass.

Renvers

FIG 34 Here the horse is bent round the outside leg for the renvers. The quarters staying on the track, the shoulders are off the track and the horse slightly bent to the outside (or in a forward direction.)

FIG 35 In the renvers seen from behind the horse's hind legs are on the track with his shoulders in from the track. The horse is bent round the rider's outside leg.

FIG 36 From above you can see clearly the bend of the horse from his tail through to his head in renvers.

Half Pass

In the half pass the forward and sideways movement of lateral work is best shown. The pronounced crossing of the outside pair of legs over and in front of the inside pair makes this one of the most exciting movements to watch.

The horse is slightly bent in the direction of movement, in the most uniform curve allowed by his conformation. His forehand leading the quarters and his head bent in the direction of movement. There are two tracks, one for the fore legs and one for the hind legs, which run parallel.

The half pass is often likened to the travers except for the relative positions of the forehand and quarters. In fact it is better compared to shoulder–in.

The rider must be careful not to let the impulsion drop in half pass, which is difficult because of the diagonal movement. In particular the inside hind may well dwell behind. The movement can be ridden at the walk but impulsion can be a problem so trot and canter are the usual paces.

Half pass

FIG 37   Here in the half pass the horse is clearly trotting forwards and sideways in good time and rhythm. There is the correct left bend although perhaps the lower jaw is a little stiff.

FIG 38   In this aerial view of the half pass the horse is bent from his tail through his back to his head, facing in the direction of movement.

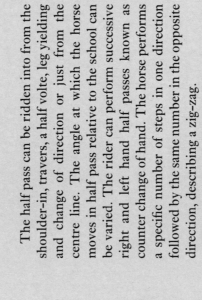

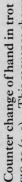

The half pass can be ridden into from the shoulder-in, travers, a half volte, leg yielding and change of direction or just from the centre line. The angle at which the horse moves in half pass relative to the school can be varied. The rider can perform successive right and left hand half passes known as counter change of hand. The horse performs a specific number of steps in one direction followed by the same number in the opposite direction, describing a zig-zag.

The number of changes of direction is only limited by the size of the arena and degree of training. The bend of the horse's body must be the same in each direction and for a moment as he changes his bend the horse must be completely straight.

Counter change of hand in trot
FIG 39 (a–e)   This sequence shows counter change of hand at trot with the horse bent to the right in the first two frames, then changing the bend and proceeding off in half pass left.

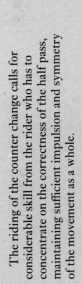

The horse must not start off in the new direction with the hindquarters leading. The forehand should always be ahead as is clearly visible in this sequence of Dutch Courage in counter change of hand at trot and subsequently canter.

The riding of the counter change calls for considerable skill from the rider who has to concentrate on the correctness of the half pass, maintaining sufficient impulsion and symmetry of the movement as a whole.

FIG 40 (a–j) Dutch
Courage in change of
hand at canter.

Counter change of hand is performed at both trot and canter, the only real difference being that at the trot the distance to which the horse moves either side of the centre line is measured in metres, while at canter it is measured in number of strides. This distance is variable depending on how many changes of hand the rider wants to complete in a given space, the angle of half pass alters accordingly.

FIG 40 (k, l) Dutch Courage still in counter change of hand continues under the camera demonstrating the bend in his body and position of the rider.

At the canter the change of hand involves a flying change, as the horse must have his leading legs towards the direction of movement. During the flying change the moment of suspension is used for the horse to readjust his sequence of footfalls. For example he will be proceeding to the left with his right hind forming beat one, his left hind and right fore are beat two and left fore beat three. During the moment of suspension he must thrust the right diagonal pair forward so that his left hind reaches the ground first to indicate the right canter.

Needless to say for the new leading legs to come 'through' properly there must be plenty of impulsion, otherwise the horse may start to swing his quarters so that the hind legs avoid stepping under him, stepping to the side instead.

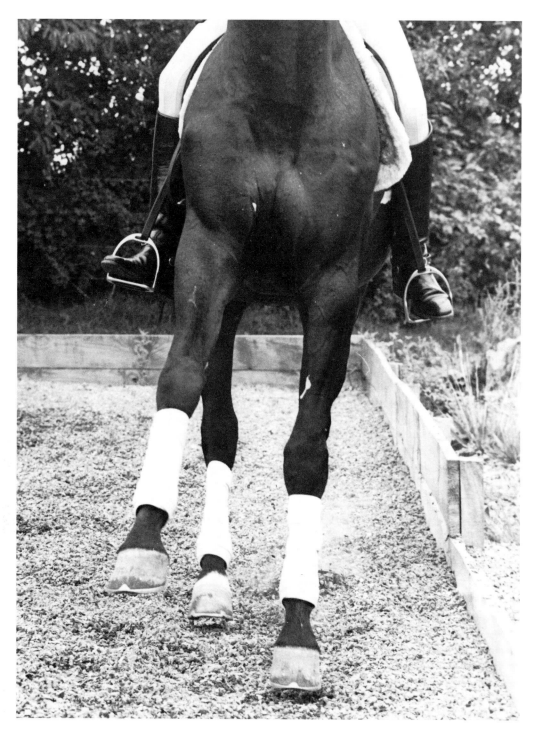

FIG 41 Here the horse is seen in the first beat of the new stride after the flying change. He has just landed on the new outside hind before the second part of the stride comes to the ground. Note the position of the rider's legs in the new right canter position.

When the horse is doing only a single change as in our example of Dutch Gold, changing from counter canter to canter right, impulsion is relatively easy to maintain. But after a half pass, where there is an inherent impulsion problem, or during sequences of changes the demands are greater.

Counter Canter and flying change
FIG 42   In (a) the rider has asked a fraction before this for the horse to change legs. During the last beat his hind legs are changing from counter canter and the hind leg has come through to take up the new right canter stride in (b). By (d) the horse shows the new right canter stride in a relaxed, collected and supple manner.

One Time Changes

There are greater demands placed on the horse's balance during multiple changes. Having completed the required number of changes the horse should be able to continue on his way without loss of rhythm. The more frequent the changes the more impulsion is required and the better the balance must be.

The trained horse can change stride as often as the rider requires, even every stride. This is shown in the Grand Prix test where fifteen single changes are executed across the diagonal of the arena. This number is specified because of the limitations of space, although horse and rider could perform many more. The horse appears to skip across the diagonal as he never makes two consecutive strides on each lead. Changes should be smooth with no jerkiness or shortening of the stride, if anything the stride should be lengthened.

One time changes

FIG 43 (a–l) In this sequence of shots Dutch Courage is proceeding across the diagonal having entered from the right rein and will leave on the left rein after a series of changes every stride.

Pirouette

The pirouette is often introduced during the early stages of training as the turn on the haunches. This involves asking the horse to move his forehand in a large circle round his quarters which describe a very small circle. The opposite in fact to the turn on the forehand.

Walk pirouette

FIG 44 (a–g) This a very good example of a walk pirouette. The horse is in a good collected walk showing heightening and shortening of the steps. His first step in the pirouette is coming slightly to the right. The hind legs are in the walk sequence but stepping in a small circle to the right with the front legs crossing. The horse maintains the right bend throughout the movement, proceeding in collected walk immediately after (g).

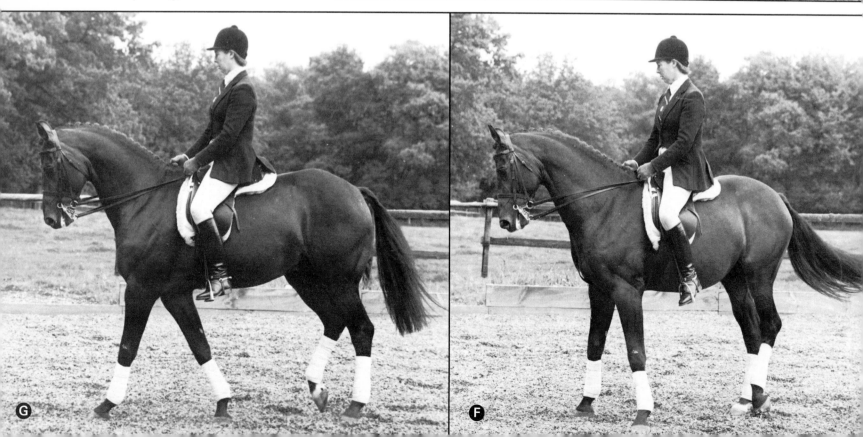

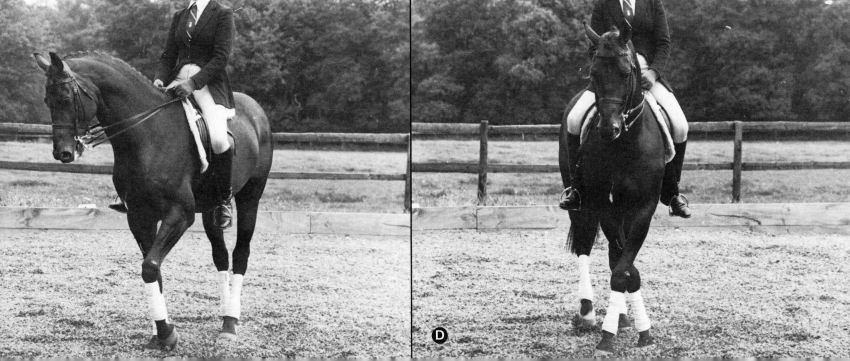

The pirouette can be performed at walk, canter and piaffe. It involves a high degree of collection which is why the piaffe is suitable but the trot is not. With the latter there is too much forward movement for the hindquarters to be able to describe a circle small enough to fit on a dinner plate, the criterion for a correct pirouette. The forehand should describe a circle the radius of which should be approximately his length. A sort of elongated half pirouette called a passada is performed at the trot but this is only used in training.

FIG 45 (a–g) This shows the walk pirouette from above. You can clearly see the bend in the horse's body during this movement. We have taken liberties with the size of the circle that the hind legs are describing in order to produce this collage shot. The circle they actually describe was much smaller.

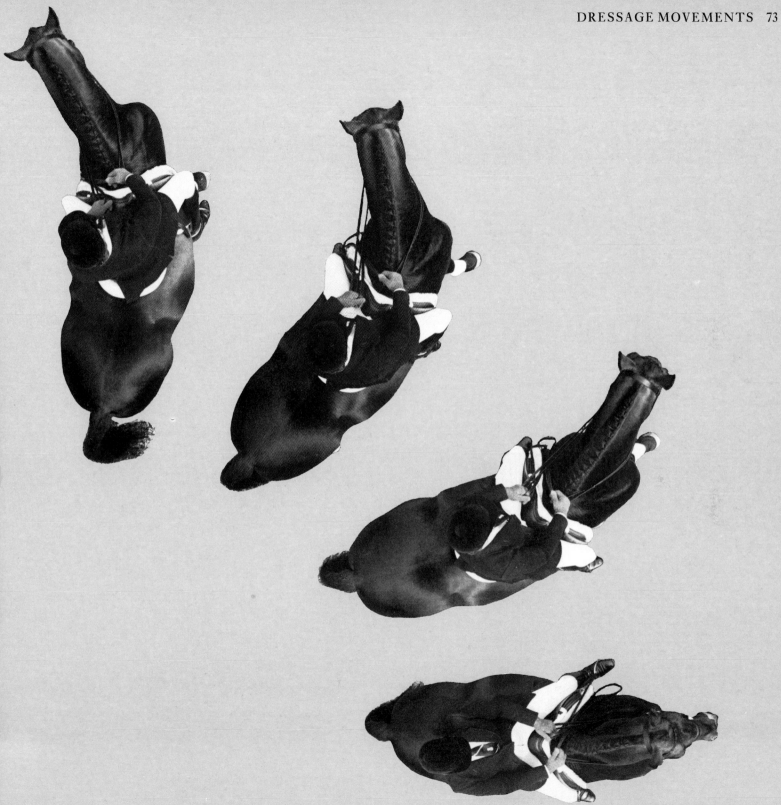

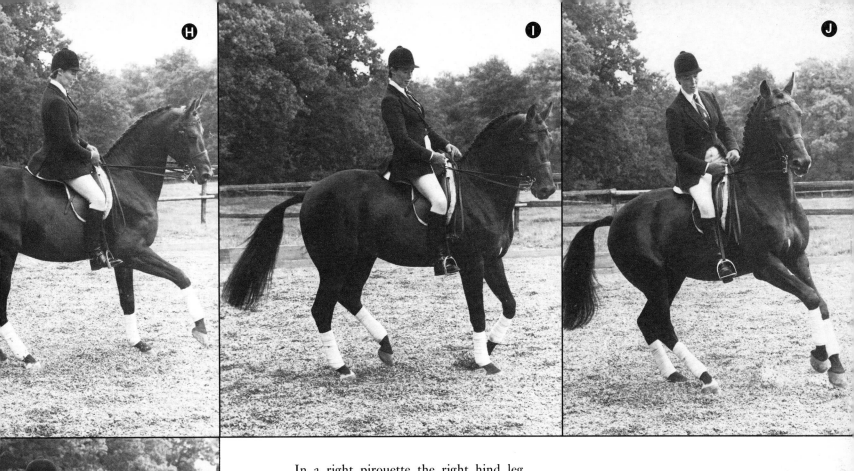

In a right pirouette the right hind leg forms the pivot, both hind legs describing a small circle, with the fore legs crossing and the horse bent in the direction of movement.

The regularity of the hoof beats is important particularly at canter where without careful attention the diagonal beat can break up and the horse fall into a four time canter. In a full 360 degree canter pirouette there should be six to eight strides. In the walk pirouette the rider has to take great care that the horse doesn't just twist his pivoting leg.

FIG 46   (a–j) 180° canter pirouette.

FIG 46 (j–n) The camera continued shooting to show the next quarter turn and Dutch Gold leaving the pirouette.

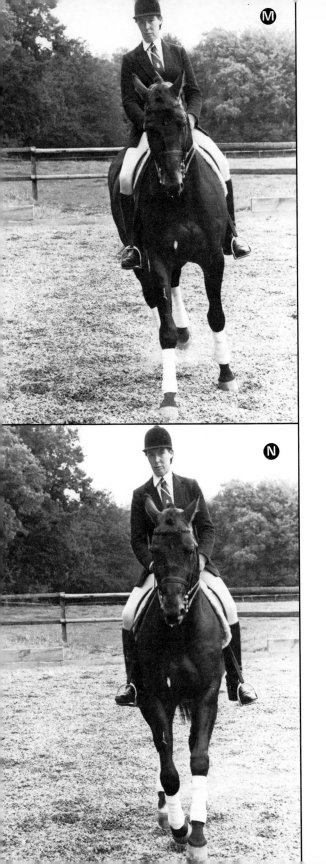

At all times the horse should remain on the bit, in balance and maintaining his rhythm. In Grand Prix tests the half pirouette (180 degrees) is performed at walk and the full pirouette (360 degrees) at canter. Although it is now becoming quite common in free style tests for people to attempt two 360 degree canter pirouettes one after another.

The half pass, single changes and pirouettes are all spectacular movements but the goal at the end of the training is the perfection of the two extremes of the trot which are the piaffe and passage. Particularly when the horse and rider can perform one after the other with ease.

FIG 47   (a–p) In the pirouette from above the
horse is correctly bent throughout. Again a little
artistic licence has been used by showing the
horse performing a circle of greater radius than
he was.

FIG 47 (g, h) These two photographs have been
enlarged bearing in mind the controversy
surrounding the question of lateral bend and
whether it is indeed possible in the horse's spine.
It is for the reader to make his own judgment.

Piaffe

The piaffe, a highly cadenced trot on the spot, is normally taught first. The legs move as diagonal pairs with an even rhythm and a definable moment of suspension. The horse should spring from one diagonal to the other, the piaffe should never appear dull and lifeless although unfortunately in competition it frequently does. The rider should aim to have the fore legs raised sufficiently so that the forearm is almost horizontal. The hoof of the suspended leg should reach the level of mid cannon bone of the leg on the ground.

In piaffe the quarters will lower and the forehand raise with the neck high and arched, giving the appearance of the horse slightly sitting down. He is in maximum collection with the quarters carrying more weight than during any other exercise. The hind legs will therefore not step as high as the fore legs but should reach above the fetlock of the foot on the ground. There should be a corresponding amount of lift between the front and back legs.

Lack of activity of the hind legs is a problem frequently seen in the competition arena. In some very bad cases the hind legs will not leave the ground and the movement is reduced to a shuffle. It is equally wrong if the hind legs move in an exaggerated way and the fore legs barely leave the ground.

When watching a horse in piaffe he should appear ready to spring forward at the slightest indication into trot or passage. The piaffe is a forward urge that has been checked, the same principle as in the rein back. Likewise there should be no rough actions on the part of the rider, often seen are harsh hands combined with plenty of spur as the rider tries to lift his or her horse from diagonal to diagonal. The whole movement should appear smooth and effortless, with no crossing of the front legs or swinging of the hindquarters.

APPENDIX

DIAGRAMS OF SCHOOL FIGURES AND LATERAL EXERCISES

DIAGRAMS NOT TO SCALE

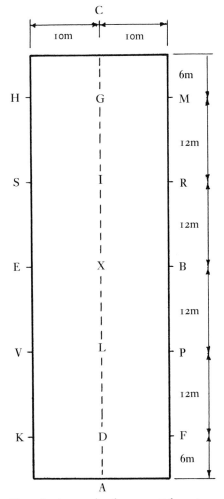

Plan of an international arena 20 × 60 metres.

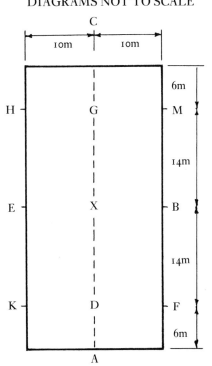

Plan of a 20 × 40 metre arena.

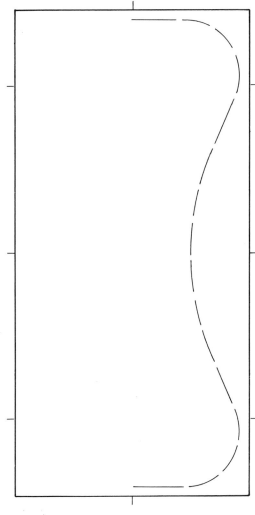

Leaving the track and returning to the track at quarter markers.

C

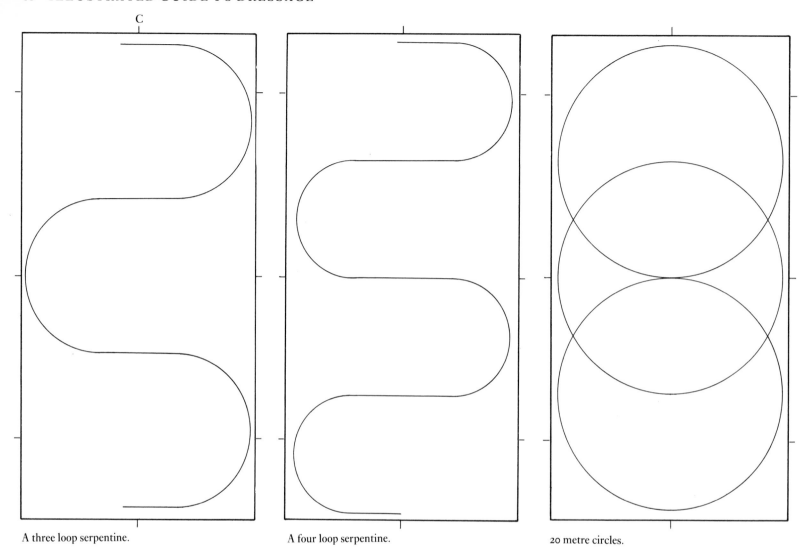

A three loop serpentine.

A four loop serpentine.

20 metre circles.

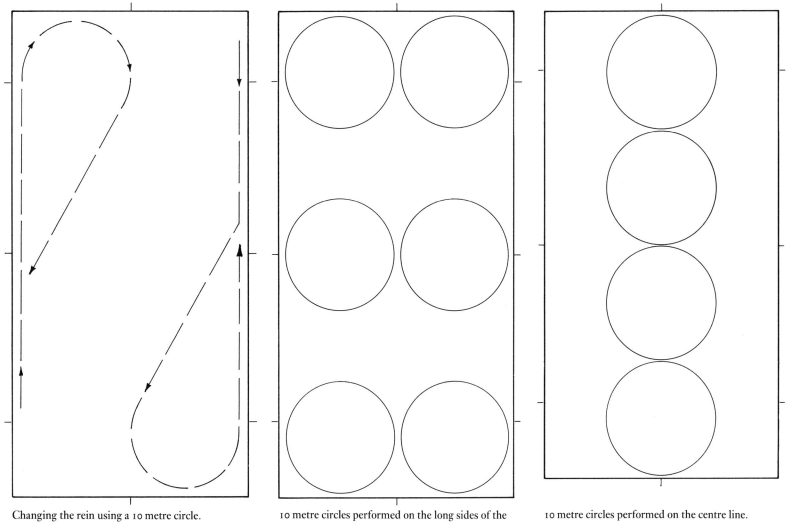

Changing the rein using a 10 metre circle.

10 metre circles performed on the long sides of the arena.

10 metre circles performed on the centre line.

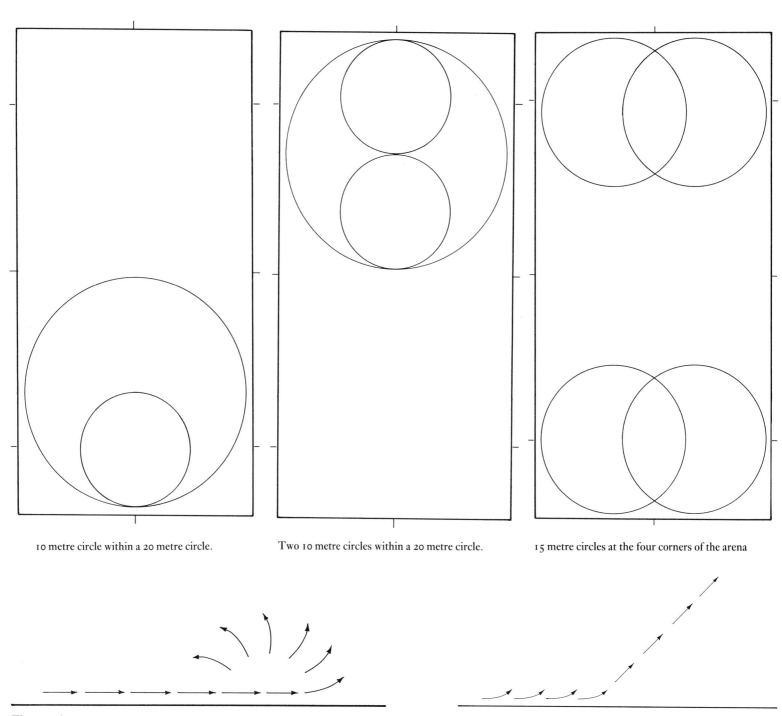

10 metre circle within a 20 metre circle.

Two 10 metre circles within a 20 metre circle.

15 metre circles at the four corners of the arena

The passada.

Shoulder in to extended trot.

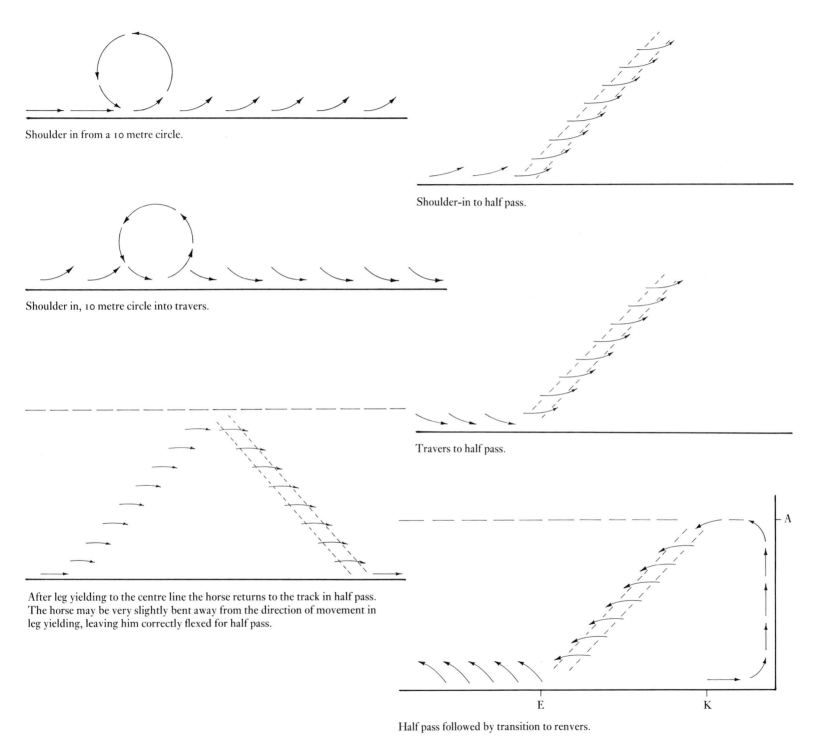

Shoulder in from a 10 metre circle.

Shoulder-in to half pass.

Shoulder in, 10 metre circle into travers.

Travers to half pass.

After leg yielding to the centre line the horse returns to the track in half pass. The horse may be very slightly bent away from the direction of movement in leg yielding, leaving him correctly flexed for half pass.

Half pass followed by transition to renvers.

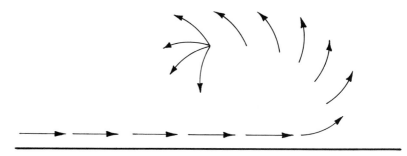

Passada into renvers to pirouette.

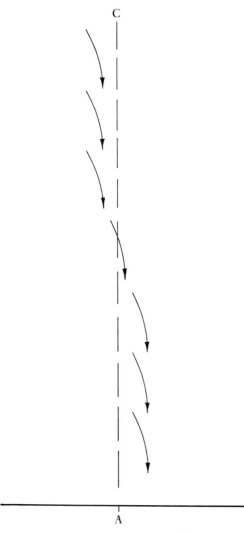

Travers across centre line into renvers.